For my curious, smart and wonderful boy, Wes. May
your years ahead bring you laughter and joy.

Love, Mommy

the Majeckles

by Regina Nay
& Alyssa Baker

Little boy Majeckle
    went to his mother
    and gave her a hug.
Mommy Majeckle chuckled,
    as this was her favorite snug.

Little boy Majeckle went outside
        to play with his dog, Jeckles.
                Jeckles had spots that
                    looked like ink blots.

Little boy Majeckle
and his dog, Jeckles,
played fetch outside and suddenly
they heard a "meow" nearby.

To their surprise,
a friendly cat came running
to join in on the playtime.
The cat meowed her name "Meckles."
Little boy Majeckle looked at his dog,
Jeckles and said, "We must tell Mommy.

Mommy Majeckle was in the kitchen making her yummy pancakes. Little boy Majeckle said, "Mommy, look, a cat named Meckles is outside! You must come quick or she might run and hide."

Mommy Majeckle with little boy
Majeckle, along with their dog,
Jeckles, quickly went outside and saw
something even more of a sight!

A bird named Peckles
was in deep conversation
with the cat, Meckles!!!

The little boy Majeckle exclaimed,
"Mommy, we must keep these
funny animals they make me laugh."
Mommy Majeckle replied,
"I certainly think that will be a good
decision. Let's take them inside".

As Mommy and little boy Majeckle walked with Jeckles, Meckles and Peckles, a frog jumped from the bush and shouted, "I'm Reckles."

"Reckles!"

Now, this was amazing
as anyone would see,
so Mommy Majeckle and
little boy Majeckle said,
"We must make our new
pets official by giving them
our last name, Majeckles!"

Just as all the Majeckles walked into their home,
Dad Majeckle came through the door, with a smile
and a laugh: he sighed and said, "You found your presents
... but there is more."

Behind Dad Majeckle
was a small cage with a mouse inside.
Dad Majeckle exclaimed,
"I could not resist
and did not want to miss out
on this little mouse named Leckles!"

Together they laughed and had dinner that night
with all their new pets, which was quite a funny sight!